In his first collection in seven years

THE INCOMPARABLE RAY BRADBURY

*conjures up eerie ghosts
of the past, present, and future
that will bewitch and disturb
his millions of readers.*

———————————•———————————

Meet the parrot to whom Hemingway confided
the plot of his last, greatest, and never-written
novel . . . The invisible ice-woman who called
herself "Melissa Toad, Witch" and offered perfect
love and a magical immunity . . . The rookie cop
who was stunned by a girl's suicide—until he
learned "her" secret.

———————————•———————————

Time passes, returns, and goes terrifyingly forward
in stories that display again "Bradbury's gift for
making you see a scene with all your senses."

—*Houston Chronicle*

———————————•———————————

"Each entry is a miniature and a jewel . . . He can
establish a mood in a line, can suggest things that
go bump in the night in soaring poetic fashion . . .
This is rainy-night stuff."

—*San Francisco Chronicle*

Long
After
Midnight

Ray
Bradbury

BANTAM BOOKS
TORONTO · NEW YORK · LONDON

*This low-priced Bantam Book
has been completely reset in a type face
designed for easy reading, and was printed
from new plates. It contains the complete
text of the original hard-cover edition.*
NOT ONE WORD HAS BEEN OMITTED.

RLI: VLM 6 (VLR 5-7)
IL 7+

LONG AFTER MIDNIGHT
*A Bantam Book / published by arrangement with
Alfred A. Knopf, Inc.*

PRINTING HISTORY
*Knopf edition published September 1976
2nd printing . . . . October 1976
Literary Guild selection September 1976*

"The Blue Bottle" Copyright 1950 by Love Romances Publishing
Inc., "Forever and the Earth" Copyright 1950 by Love
Romances Publishing Inc., "Punishment Without Crime" Copy-
right 1950 by Other Worlds, "The Miracles of Jamie" first
appeared in Charm, "The October Game" in Weird Tales,
"One Timeless Spring" and "The Pumpernickel" in Collier's,
"A Piece of Wood" in Esquire, "The Utterly Perfect Murder"
("My Perfect Murder") and "The Parrot Who Met Papa" in
Playboy Magazine, "Have I Got a Chocolate Bar for You!" in
Penthouse, "The Wish" in Woman's Day Magazine, and "Drink
Entire: Against the Madness of Crowds" in Gallery.

Bantam edition / April 1978

This book, with love,
is dedicated to William F. Nolan,
amazing collector, fantastic
researcher, dear friend.

Contents

CONTENTS

Long After Midnight

The Blue Bottle

The sundials were tumbled into white pebbles. The birds of the air now flew in ancient skies of rock and sand, buried, their songs stopped. The dead sea bottoms were currented with dust which flooded the land when the wind bade it reenact an old tale of engulfment. The cities were deep laid with granaries of silence, time stored and kept, pools and fountains of quietude and memory.

Mars was dead.

Then, out of the large stillness, from a great distance, there was an insect sound which grew large among the cinnamon hills and moved in the sun-blazed air until the highway trembled and dust was shook whispering down in the old cities.

The sound ceased.

In the shimmering silence of midday, Albert Beck and Leonard Craig sat in an ancient landcar, eyeing a dead city which did not move under their gaze but waited for their shout:

"Hello!"

A crystal tower dropped into soft dusting rain.

"You there!"

And another tumbled down.

And another and another fell as Beck called, summoning them to death. In shattering flights, stone animals with vast granite wings dived to strike the courtyards and fountains. His cry summoned them like living beasts and the beasts gave answer, groaned, cracked, leaned up, tilted over, trembling, hesitant, then split the air and swept down with grimaced mouths and empty eyes, with sharp, eternally hungry teeth suddenly seized out and strewn like shrapnel on the tiles.

Beck waited. No more towers fell.

"It's safe to go in now."

Craig didn't move. "For the same reason?"

Beck nodded.

"For a damned *bottle!* I don't understand. Why does everyone want it?"

Beck got out of the car. "Those that found it, they never told, they never explained. But—it's old. Old as the desert, as the dead seas—and it might contain anything. That's what the legend says. And because it *could* hold anything—well, that stirs a man's hunger."

"Yours, not mine," said Craig. His mouth barely moved; his eyes were half-shut, faintly amused. He stretched lazily. "I'm just along for the ride. Better watching you than sitting in the heat."

Beck had stumbled upon the old landcar a month back, before Craig had joined him. It was part of the flotsam of the First Industrial Invasion of Mars that had ended when the race moved on toward the stars. He had worked on the motor and run it from city to dead city, through the lands of the idlers and roustabouts, the dreamers and lazers, men caught in the backwash of space, men like himself and Craig who had never wanted to do much of anything and had found Mars a fine place to do it in.

"Five thousand, ten thousand years back the Martians

made the Blue Bottle," said Beck. "Blown from Martian glass—and lost and found and lost and found again and again."

He stared into the wavering heat shimmer of the dead city. All my life, thought Beck, I've done nothing and nothing inside the nothing. Others, better men, have done big things, gone off to Mercury, or Venus, or out beyond the System. Except me. Not me. But the Blue Bottle can *change* all that.

He turned and walked away from the silent car.

Craig was out and after him, moving easily along. "What is it now, ten years you've hunted? You twitch when you sleep, wake up in fits, sweat through the days. You want the damn bottle *that* bad, and don't know what's in it. You're a fool, Beck."

"Shut up, shut up," said Beck, kicking a slide of pebbles out of his way.

They walked together into the ruined city, over a mosaic of cracked tiles shaped into a stone tapestry of fragile Martian creatures, long-dead beasts which appeared and disappeared as a slight breath of wind stirred the silent dust.

"Wait," said Beck. He cupped his hands to his mouth and gave a great shout. "You there!"

". . . there," said an echo, and towers fell. Fountains and stone pillars folded into themselves. That was the way of these cities. Sometimes towers as beautiful as a symphony would fall at a spoken word. It was like watching a Bach cantata disintegrate before your eyes.

A moment later: bones buried in bones. The dust settled. Two structures remained intact.

Beck stepped forward, nodding to his friend.

They moved in search.

And, searching, Craig paused, a faint smile on his lips. "In that bottle," he said, "is there a little accordion woman, all folded up like one of those tin cups, or like one of those Japanese flowers you put in water and it opens out?"

"I don't need a woman."

"Maybe you do. Maybe you never had a *real* woman, a woman who loved you, so, secretly, that's what you hope is in it." Craig pursed his mouth. "Or maybe, in that bottle, something from your childhood. All in a tiny bundle—a lake, a tree you climbed, green grass, some crayfish. How's *that* sound?"

Beck's eyes focused on a distant point. "Sometimes— that's almost it. The past—Earth. I don't know."

Craig nodded. "What's in the bottle would depend, maybe, on who's looking. Now, if there was a shot of *whiskey* in it . . ."

"Keep looking," said Beck.

There were seven rooms filled with glitter and shine; from floor to tiered ceiling there were casks, crocks, magnums, urns, vases—fashioned of red, pink, yellow, violet, and black glass. Beck shattered them, one by one, to eliminate them, to get them out of the way so he would never have to go through them again.

Beck finished his room, stood ready to invade the next. He was almost afraid to go on. Afraid that *this* time he would find it; that the search would be over and the meaning would go out of his life. Only after he had heard of the Blue Bottle from fire-travelers all the way from Venus to Jupiter, ten years ago, had life begun to take on a purpose. The fever had lit him and he had burned steadily ever since. If he worked it properly, the prospect of finding the bottle might fill his entire life to the brim. Another thirty years, if he was careful and not *too* diligent, of search, never admitting aloud that it wasn't the bottle that counted at all, but the search, the running and the hunting, the dust and the cities and the going-on.

Beck heard a muffled sound. He turned and walked to a window looking out into the courtyard. A small gray sand cycle had purred up almost noiselessly at the end of the street. A plump man with blond hair eased himself off the spring seat and stood looking into the city. Another searcher. Beck sighed. Thousands of them, searching and searching. But there were thousands of brittle cities and towns and villages and it would take a millennium to sift them all.

"How you doing?" Craig appeared in a doorway.

"No luck." Beck sniffed the air. "Do you smell anything?"

"What?" Craig looked about.

"Smells like—bourbon."

"Ho!" Craig laughed. "That's *me!*"

"You?"

"I just took a drink. Found it in the other room. Shoved some stuff around, a mess of bottles, like always, and one of them had some bourbon in it, so I had myself a drink."

Beck was staring at him, beginning to tremble. "What—what would bourbon be doing *here*, in a Martian bottle?" His hands were cold. He took a slow step forward. "Show me!"

"I'm sure that . . ."

"*Show* me, damn you!"

It was there, in one corner of the room, a container of Martian glass as blue as the sky, the size of a small fruit, light and airy in Beck's hand as he set it down upon a table.

"It's half-full of bourbon," said Craig.

"I don't see anything inside," said Beck.

"Then shake it."

Beck picked it up, gingerly shook it.

"Hear it gurgle?"

"No."

"I can hear it plain."

Beck replaced it on the table. Sunlight spearing through a side window struck blue flashes off the slender container. It was the blue of a star held in the hand. It was the blue of a shallow ocean bay at noon. It was the blue of a diamond at morning.

"This *is* it," said Beck quietly. "I know it is. We don't have to look anymore. We've found the Blue Bottle."

Craig looked skeptical. "Sure you don't *see* anything in it?"

"Nothing . . . But—" Beck bent close and peered deeply into the blue universe of glass. "Maybe if I open it up and let it out, whatever it is, I'll know."

"I put the stopper in tight. Here." Craig reached out.

"If you gentlemen will excuse me," said a voice in the door behind them.

The plump man with blond hair walked into their line of vision with a gun. He did not look at their faces, he looked only at the blue glass bottle. He began to smile. "I hate very much to handle guns," he said, "but it is a matter of necessity, as I simply *must* have that work of art. I suggest that you allow me to take it without trouble."

Beck was almost pleased. It had a certain beauty of timing, this incident; it was the sort of thing he might have wished for, to have the treasure stolen before it was opened. Now there was the good prospect of a chase, a fight, a series of gains and losses, and, before they were done, perhaps another four or five years spent upon a new search.

"Come along now," said the stranger. "Give it up." He raised the gun warningly.

Beck handed him the bottle.

"Amazing. Really amazing," said the plump man. "I can't believe it was as simple as this, to walk in, hear two men talking, and to have the Blue Bottle simply *handed* to me. Amazing!" And he wandered off down the hall, out into the daylight, chuckling to himself.

Under the cool double moons of Mars the midnight cities were bone and dust. Along the scattered highway the landcar bumped and rattled, past cities where the fountains, the gyrostats, the furniture, the metal-singing books, the paintings lay powdered over with mortar and insect wings. Past cities that were cities no longer, but only things rubbed to a fine silt that flowered senselessly back and forth on the wine winds between one land and another, like the sand in a gigantic hourglass, endlessly pyramiding and repyramiding. Silence opened to let the car pass, and closed swiftly in behind.

Craig said, "We'll never find him. These damned roads. So old. Potholes, lumps, everything wrong. He's got the advantage with the cycle; he can dodge and weave. Damn!"

They swerved abruptly, avoiding a bad stretch. The car moved over the old highway like an eraser, coming upon blind soil, passing over it, dusting it away to reveal the emerald and gold color of ancient Martian mosaics worked into the road surface.

"Wait," cried Beck. He throttled the car down. "I saw something back there."

"Where?"

They drove back a hundred yards.

"There. You see. It's *him*."

In a ditch by the side of the road the plump man lay folded over his cycle. He did not move. His eyes were wide, and when Beck flashed a torch down, the eyes burned dully.

"Where's the bottle?" asked Craig.

Beck jumped into the ditch and picked up the man's gun. "I don't know. Gone."

"What killed him?"

"I don't know that either."

"The cycle looks okay. Not an accident."

Beck rolled the body over. "No wounds. Looks like he just—stopped, of his own accord."

"Heart attack, maybe," said Craig. "Excited over the bottle. He gets down here to hide. Thought he'd be all right, but the attack finished him."

"That doesn't account for the Blue Bottle."

"Someone came along. Lord, you know how many searchers there are. . . ."

They scanned the darkness around them. Far off, in the starred blackness, on the blue hills, they saw a dim movement.

"Up there." Beck pointed. "Three men on foot."

"They must have . . ."

"My God, look!"

Below them, in the ditch, the figure of the plump man glowed, began to melt. The eyes took on the aspect of moonstones under a sudden rush of water. The face began to dissolve away into fire. The hair resembled small firecracker strings, lit and sputtering. The body fumed as they watched. The fingers jerked with flame. Then, as if a gigantic hammer had struck a glass statue, the body cracked upward and was gone in a blaze of pink shards, becoming mist as the night breeze carried it across the highway.

"They must have—*done* something to him," said Craig. "Those three, with a new kind of weapon."

"But it's happened before," said Beck. "Men I knew about who had the Blue Bottle. They vanished. And the bottle passed on to others who vanished." He shook his head. "Looked like a million fireflies when he broke apart. . . ."

"You going after them?"

Beck returned to the car. He judged the desert mounds, the hills of bone-silt and silence. "It'll be a tough job, but I think I can poke the car through after them. I *have* to, now." He paused, not speaking to Craig. "I think I know what's in the Blue Bottle. . . . Finally, I realize that what I want most of all is in there. Waiting for me."

"I'm not going," said Craig, coming up to the car where Beck sat in the dark, his hands on his knees. "I'm not going out there with you, chasing three armed men. I just want to live, Beck. That bottle means nothing to me. I won't risk my skin for it. But I'll wish you luck."

"Thanks," said Beck. And he drove away, into the dunes.

* * *

The night was as cool as water coming over the glass hood of the landcar.

Beck throttled hard over dead river washes and spills of chalked pebble, driving between great cliffs. Ribbons of double moonlight painted the bas-reliefs of gods and animals on the cliff sides all yellow gold: mile-high faces upon which Martian histories were etched and stamped in symbols, incredible faces with open cave eyes and gaping cave mouths.

The motor's roar dislodged rocks, boulders. In a whole rushing downpour of stone, golden segments of ancient cliff sculpture slid out of the moons' rays at the top of the cliff and vanished into blue cool-well darkness.

In the roar, as he drove, Beck cast his mind back—to all the nights in the last ten years, nights when he had built red fires on the sea bottoms, and cooked slow, thoughtful meals. And dreamed. Always those dreams of *wanting*. And not knowing what. Ever since he was a young man, the hard life on Earth, the great panic of 2130, the starvation, chaos, riot, want. Then bucking through the planets, the womanless, loveless years, the alone years. You come out of the dark into the light, out of the womb into the world, and what do you find that you really want?

What about that dead man back there in the ditch? Wasn't he always looking for something extra? Something he didn't have. What *was* there for men like himself? Or for anyone? Was there anything at all to look forward to?

The Blue Bottle.

He quickly braked the car, leaped out, gun ready. He ran, crouching, into the dunes. Ahead of him, the three men lay on the cold sand, neatly. They were Earthmen, with tan faces and rough clothes and gnarled hands. Starlight shone on the Blue Bottle, which lay among them.

As Beck watched, the bodies began to melt. They vanished away into rises of steam, into dewdrops and crystals. In a moment they were gone.

Beck felt the coldness in his body as the flakes rained across his eyes, flicking his lips and his cheeks.

He did not move.

The plump man. Dead and vanishing. Craig's voice: "Some new weapon . . ."

No. Not a weapon at all.

The Blue Bottle.

They had opened it to find what they most desired. All of the unhappy, desiring men down the long lonely years had opened it to find what they most wanted in the planets of the universe. And all had found it, even as had these three. Now it could be understood, why the bottle passed on so swiftly, from one to another, and the men vanishing behind it. Harvest chaff fluttering on the sand, along the dead sea rims. Turning to flame and fireflies. To mist.

Beck picked up the bottle and held it away from himself for a long moment. His eyes shone clearly. His hands trembled.

So this is what I've been looking for, he thought. He turned the bottle and it flashed blue starlight.

So this is what all men *really* want? The secret desire, deep inside, hidden all away where we never guess? The subliminal urge? So this is what each man seeks, through some private guilt, to find?

Death.

An end to doubt, to torture, to monotony, to want, to loneliness, to fear, an end to everything.

All men?

No. Not Craig. Craig was, perhaps, far luckier. A few men were like animals in the universe, not questioning, drinking at pools and breeding and raising their young and not doubting for a moment that life was anything but good. That was Craig. There were a handful like him. Happy animals on a great reservation, in the hand of God, with a religion and a faith that grew like a set of special nerves in them. The unneurotic men in the midst of the billionfold neurotics.

They would only want death, later, in a natural manner. Not now. Later.

Beck raised the bottle. How simple, he thought, and how right. This *is* what I've always wanted. And nothing else.

Nothing.

The bottle was open and blue in the starlight. Beck took an immense draught of the air coming from the Blue Bottle, deep into his lungs.

I have it at last, he thought.

He relaxed. He felt his body become wonderfully cool and then wonderfully warm. He knew he was dropping down a long slide of stars into a darkness as delightful as wine. He was swimming in blue wine and white wine and red wine. There were candles in his chest, and fire wheels spinning. He felt his hands leave him. He felt his legs fly away, amusingly. He laughed. He shut his eyes and laughed.

He was very happy for the first time in his life.

The Blue Bottle dropped onto the cool sand.

At dawn, Craig walked along, whistling. He saw the bottle lying in the first pink light of the sun on the empty white sand. As he picked it up, there was a fiery whisper. A number of orange and red-purple fireflies blinked on the air, and passed on away.

The place was very still.

"I'll be damned." He glanced toward the dead windows of a nearby city. "Hey, Beck!"

A slender tower collapsed into powder.

"Beck, here's your treasure! I don't want it. Come and get it!"

". . . and get it," said an echo, and the last tower fell.

Craig waited.

"That's rich," he said. "The bottle right here, and old Beck not even around to take it." He shook the blue container.

It gurgled.

"Yes, sir! Just the way it was before. Full of bourbon, by God!" He opened it, drank, wiped his mouth.

He held the bottle carelessly.

"All that trouble for a little bourbon. I'll wait right here for old Beck and give him his damn bottle. Meanwhile—have another drink, Mr. Craig. Don't mind if I do."

The only sound in the dead land was the sound of liquid running into a parched throat. The Blue Bottle flashed in the sun.

Craig smiled happily and drank again.

One Timeless Spring

That week, so many years ago, I thought my mother and father were poisoning me. And now, twenty years later, I'm not so sure they didn't. There's no way of telling.

It all comes back to me through the simple expedient of an examined trunk in the attic. This morning I pulled back the brass hasps and lifted the lid, and the immemorial odor of mothballs shrouded the unstrung tennis rackets, the worn sneakers, the shattered toys, the rusty roller skates. These implements of play, seen again through older eyes, make it seem only an hour ago that I rushed in from the shady streets, all asweat, the cry of "Ollie, Ollie, Oxen Free!" still excitedly trembling on my lips.

I was a weird and ridiculous boy then with brooding and uncommon ideas; the poison and the fear were only part of me in those years. I began making notes in a lined nickel tablet when I was only twelve. I can feel

the stubby pencil in my fingers now, writing in those
timeless mornings.

I paused to lick my pencil, thoughtfully. I sat in my
upstairs room at the beginning of a clear endless day,
blinking at the rose-stamped wallpaper, my feet bare,
my hair shorn to a hairbrush stubble, thinking.

"I didn't know I was sick until this week," I wrote.
"I've been sick for a long time. Since I was ten. I'm
twelve now."

I scrouged up my face, bit my lips hard, focused
blurrily on the tablet. "Mom and Dad have *made* me
sick. Teachers at school also gave this—" I hesitated.
Then I wrote: "*Disease* to me! The only ones who
don't scare me are the other kids. Isabel Skelton and
Willard Bowers and Clarisse Mellin; they aren't very
sick yet. But I'm *really* bad off. . . ."

I laid the pencil down. I went to the bathroom mirror
to see myself. My mother called me from downstairs to
come to breakfast. I pressed close to the mirror, breath-
ing so fast I made a big damp fog on the glass. I saw
how my face was—changing.

The bones of it. Even the eyes. The pores of my
nose. My ears. My forehead. My hair. All the things
that'd been me for such a long time, starting to become something else. ("Douglas, come to breakfast,
you'll be late for school!") As I took a quick wash I
saw my body floating under me. I was inside it. There
was no escape. And the bones of it were doing things,
shifting, mixing around!

Then I began singing and whistling loud, so I
wouldn't think about it; until Father, rapping on the
door, told me to quiet down and come eat.

I sat at the breakfast table. There was a yellow box
of cereal and milk, white-cold in a pitcher, and shining
spoons and knives, and eggs planked with bacon, Dad
reading his paper, Mom moving around the kitchen. I
sniffed. I felt my stomach lie down like a whipped dog.

"What's wrong, son?" Dad looked at me casually. "Not hungry?"

"No, sir."

"A boy should be hungry in the morning," said Father.

"You go ahead and eat," said Mother at me. "Go on now. Hurry."

I looked at the eggs. They were poison. I looked at the butter. It was poison. The milk was so white and creamy and poisonous in its pitcher, and the cereal was brown and crisp and tasty in a green dish with pink flowers on it.

Poison, all of them, poison! The thought ran in my head like ants at a picnic. I caught my lip in my teeth.

"Unh?" said Dad, blinking at me. You *said?*"

"Nothing," I said. "Except I'm not hungry."

I couldn't say I was ill and that food made me ill. I couldn't say that cookies, cakes, cereals and soups and vegetables had done *this* to me, could I? No, I had to sit, swallowing nothing, my heart beginning to pound.

"Well, drink your milk at least, and go on," said Mother. "Dad, give him money for a good lunch at school. Orange juice, meat, and milk. No candy."

She didn't have to warn me on candy. It was worst of all the poisons. I wouldn't touch it again, ever!

I strapped my books and went to the door.

"Douglas, you didn't kiss me," said Mom.

"Oh," I said, and shuffled to kiss her.

"What's wrong with you?" she asked.

"Nothing," I said. " 'Bye. So long, Dad."

Everybody said good-bye. I walked to school, thinking deep inside, like shouting down a long, cold well.

I ran down through the ravine and swung on a vine, way out; the ground dropped away, I smelled the cool morning air, sweet and high, and I screamed with laughter, and the wind threw away my thoughts. I tossed myself in a flip-against the embankment and rolled down as birds whistled at me and a squirrel hopped like brown fuzz blown by the wind up around a tree trunk. Down the path the other kids fell like a small avalanche, yelling. "Ahh—eee—yah!" Pounding their chests, skipping rocks on the water, jumping their hands down to catch at crayfish. The crayfish jetted away in dusty spurts. We all laughed and joked.

A girl passed by on the green wooden bridge above us. Her name was Clarisse Mellin. We all hee-hawed at her, told her to go on, go on, we didn't want her with us, go on, go on! But my voice caught and trailed off, and I watched her going, slowly. I didn't look away.

From way off in the morning we heard the school bell ring.

We scrambled up trails we'd made during many summers over the years. The grass was worn; we knew each snake hole and bump, each tree, every vine, every weed of it. After school we'd made tree huts here, high up over the shining creek, jumped in the water naked, gone on long hikes down the ravine to where it emptied lonely and abandoned into the big blue of Lake Michigan, near the tannery and the asbestos works and the docks.

Now, as we panted up to school, I stopped, afraid again. "You go on ahead," I said.

The last bell tolled. The kids ran. I looked at the school with vines growing on it. I heard the voices inside, making a high, all-the-time noise. I heard little desk bells tinkle and sharp teacher voices reaching out.

Poison, I thought. The teachers, too! They want me sick! They teach you how to be sicker and sicker! And —and how to *enjoy* being sick!

"Good morning, Douglas."

I heard high-heeled shoes on the cement walk. Miss Adams, the principal, with her pince-nez and wide, pale face and close-cropped dark hair, stood behind me.

"Come along in," she said, holding my shoulder firmly. "You're late. Come along."

She guided me, one two, one two, one two, upstairs, up the stairs to my fate. . . .

Mr. Jordan was a plump man with thinning hair and serious green eyes and a way of rocking on his heels before his charts. Today he had a large illustration of a body with all its skin off. Exposed were green, blue, pink, and yellow veins, capillaries, muscles, tendons, organs, lungs, bones, and fatty tissues.

Mr. Jordon nodded before the chart. "There's a great similarity between cancer and normal cell reproduction. Cancer is simply a normal function gone wild. Overproduction of cellular material—"

I raised my hand. "How does food—I mean—what makes the body grow?"

"A good question, Douglas." He tapped the chart. "Food, taken into the body, is broken down, assimilated, and—"

I listened and I knew what Mr. Jordan was trying to do to me. My childhood was in my mind like a fossil imprint on soft shale rock. Mr. Jordan was trying to polish and smooth it away. Eventually it would be all gone, all my beliefs and imaginings. My mother changed my body with food, Mr. Jordan worked on my mind with words.

So I began to draw pictures on paper, not listening. I hummed little songs, made up a language all my own. The rest of the day I heard nothing. I resisted the attack, I counteracted the poison.

But then after school I passed Mrs. Singer's store and I bought candy. I couldn't help it. And after I ate it I wrote on the back of the wrapper: "This is the last candy I'm going to eat. Even at the Saturday matinee, when Tom Mix comes on the screen with Tony, I won't eat candy again."

I looked at the candy bars stacked like a harvest on the shelves. Orange wrappers with sky-blue words saying "Chocolate." Yellow and violet wrappers with blue words on them. I felt the candy in my body, making my cells grow. Mrs. Singer sold hundreds of candy bars each day. Was she in conspiracy? Did she know what she was doing to children with them? Was she jealous of them being so young? Did she want them to grow old? I wanted to kill her!

"What you doing?"

Bill Arno had come up behind me while I was writing on the candy wrapper. Clarisse Mellin was with him. She looked at me with her blue eyes and said nothing.

I hid the paper. "Nothing," I said.

We all walked along. We saw kids playing hopscotch and kick the can and playing mibs on the hard ground, and I turned to Bill and I said, "We won't be allowed to do that next year, or maybe the year after."

Bill only laughed and said, "Sure, we will. Who'll stop us?"

"*They* will," I said.

"Who's they?" asked Bill.

"Never mind," I said. "Just wait and see."

"Aw," said Bill. "You're crazy."

"You don't understand!" I cried. "You play and run around and eat, and all the time they're tricking you and making you think different and act different and walk different. And all of a sudden one day you'll stop playing and have to worry!" My face was hot and my hands were clenched. I was blind with rage. Bill turned, laughing, and walked away. "Over Annie Over!" someone sang, tossing a ball over a housetop.

You might go all day without breakfast or lunch, but what about supper? My stomach shouted as I slid into my chair at the supper table. I held on to my knees, looking down at them. I won't eat, I told myself. I'll show them. I'll fight them.

Dad pretended to be considerate. "Let him go without supper," he said to my mother, when he saw me neglect my food. He winked at her. "He'll eat later."

All evening long I played on the warm brick streets of town, rattling the tin cans and climbing the trees in the growing dark.

Coming into the kitchen at ten o'clock, I realized it was no use. There was a note on top of the icebox which said, "Help yourself. Dad."

I opened the refrigerator, and a little cool breath breathed out against me, cold, with the smell of rimed foods on it. Inside was the wondrous half-ruin of a chicken. Members of celery were piled like cords of wood. Strawberries grew in a thicket of parsley.

My hands blurred. They made motions that caused an illusion of a dozen hands. Like those pictures of Eastern goddesses they worship in temples. One hand with a tomato in it. One hand grasping a banana. A third hand seizing strawberries! A fourth, fifth, sixth hand caught in midmotion, each with a bit of cheese, olive, or radish!

Half an hour later I knelt by the toilet bowl and swiftly raised the seat. Then, rapidly, I opened my mouth, and shoved a spoon back, back along my tongue, down, down along my gagging throat. . . .

Lying in bed, I shuddered and tasted the acrid memory in my mouth, glad to be rid of the food I had so eagerly swallowed. I hated myself for my weakness. I lay trembling, empty, hungry again, but too sick, now, to eat. . . .

I was very weak in the morning, and noticeably pale, for my mother made a comment on it. "If you're not better by Monday," she said, "to the doctor's with you!"

It was Saturday. The day of shouting, and no tiny little silver bells for teachers to silence it; the day when the colorless giants moved on the pale screen at the Elite movie house in the long theater dark, and children were only children, and not things growing.

I saw no one. In the morning when I should have been hiking out along the North Shore Rail Line, where the hot sun simmered up from the long parallels of metal, I lolled about in terrific indecision. And by the time I got to the ravine it was already midafternoon and it was deserted; all of the kids had run downtown to see the matinee and suck lemon drops.

The ravine was very alone, it looked so undisturbed and old and green, I was a little afraid of it. I had never seen it so quiet. The vines hung quietly upon the trees and the water went over the rocks and the birds sang high up.

I went down the secret trail, hiding behind bushes, pausing, going on.

Clarisse Mellin was crossing the bridge as I reached it. She was coming home from town with some little packages under her arm. We said hello, self-consciously.

"What are you doing?" she asked.

"Oh, walking around," I said.

"All alone?"

"Yeah. All the other guys are downtown."

She hesitated, then said, "Can I walk with you?"

"I guess so," I said. "Come on."

We walked down through the ravine. It was humming like a big dynamo. Nothing seemed to want to move, everything was quiet. Pink darning needles flew and bumped on air pockets, and hovered over the sparkling creek water.

Clarisse's hand bumped mine as we walked along the trail. I smelled the moist dank smell of the ravine and the soft new smell of Clarisse beside me.

We came to a place where there was a cross trail.

"We built a tree hut up there last year," I said, pointing.

"Where?" Clarisse stepped close to me to see where my finger was pointing. "I don't see."

"There," I said, my voice breaking, and pointed again.

Very quietly, she put her arm around me. I was so surprised and bewildered I almost cried out. Then, trembling, her lips kissed me, and my own hands were moving to hold her and I was shaking and shouting inside myself.

The silence was like a green explosion. The water bubbled on in the creek bed. I couldn't breathe.

I knew it was all over. I was lost. From this moment on, it would be a touching, an eating of foods, a learning of language and algebra and logic, a movement and an emotion, a kissing and a holding, a whirl of feeling that caught and sucked me drowning under. I knew I was lost forever now, and I didn't care. But I *did* care, and I was laughing and crying all in one, and there was nothing to do about it, but hold her and love her with all my decided and rioting body and mind.

I could have gone on fighting my war against Mother and Dad and school and food and things in books, but I couldn't fight this sweetness on my lips and this warmness in my hands, and the new odor in my nostrils.

"Clarisse, Clarisse," I cried, holding her, looking over her shoulder blindly, whispering to her. "Clarisse!"

The Parrot Who Met Papa

The kidnaping was reported all around the world, of course.

It took a few days for the full significance of the news to spread from Cuba to the United States, to the Left Bank in Paris and then finally to some small good café in Pamplona where the drinks were fine and the weather, somehow, was always just right.

But once the meaning of the news really hit, people were on the phone, Madrid was calling New York, New York was shouting south at Havana to verify, please verify this crazy thing.

And then some woman in Venice, Italy, with a blurred voice called through, saying she was at Harry's Bar that very instant and was destroyed, this thing that had happened was terrible, a cultural heritage was placed in immense and irrevocable danger. . . .

Not an hour later, I got a call from a baseball pitcher—*cum*-novelist who had been a great friend of Papa's and who now lived in Madrid half the year and Nairobi the rest. He was in tears, or sounded close to it.

"Tell me," he said, from halfway around the world, "what happened? What are the facts?"

Well, the facts were these: Down in Havana, Cuba, about fourteen kilometers from Papa's Finca Vigía home, there is a bar in which he used to drink. It is the one where they named a special drink for him, not the fancy one where he used to meet flashy literary lights such as K-K-Kenneth Tynan and, er, Tennessee W-Williams (as Mr. Tynan would say it). No, it is not the Floridita; it is a shirt-sleeves place with plain wooden tables, sawdust on the floor, and a big mirror like a dirty cloud behind the bar. Papa went there when there were too many tourists around the Floridita who wanted to meet Mr. Hemingway. And the thing that happened there was destined to be big news, bigger than the report of what he said to Fitzgerald about the rich, even bigger than the story of his swing at Max Eastman on that long-ago day in Charlie Scribner's office. This news had to do with an ancient parrot.

That senior bird lived in a cage right atop the bar in the Cuba Libre. He had "kept his cage" in that place for roughly twenty-nine years, which means that the old parrot had been there almost as long as Papa had lived in Cuba.

And that adds up to this monumental fact: All during the time Papa had lived in Finca Vigía, he had known the parrot and had talked to him and the parrot had talked back. As the years passed, people said that Hemingway began to talk like the parrot and others said no, the parrot learned to talk like *him!* Papa used to line the drinks up on the counter and sit near the cage and involve that bird in the best kind of conversation you ever heard, four nights running. By the end of the second year, that parrot knew more about Hem and Thomas Wolfe and Sherwood Anderson than Gertrude Stein did. In fact, the parrot even knew who Gertrude

Stein *was*. All you had to say was "Gertrude" and the parrot said:

"Pigeons on the grass alas."

At the other times, pressed, the parrot would say, "There was this old man and this boy and this boat and this sea and this big fish in the sea. . . ." And then it would take time out to eat a cracker.

Well, this fabled creature, this parrot, this odd bird, vanished, cage and all, from the Cuba Libre late one Sunday afternoon.

And that's why my phone was ringing itself off the hook. And that's why one of the big magazines got a special State Department clearance and flew me down to Cuba to see if I could find so much as the cage, anything remaining of the bird or anyone resembling a kidnaper. They wanted a light and amiable article, with overtones, as they said. And, very honestly, I was curious. I had heard rumors of the bird. In a strange kind of way, I was concerned.

I got off the jet from Mexico City and taxied straight across Havana to that strange little café-bar.

I almost failed to get in the place. As I stepped through the door, a dark little man jumped up from a chair and cried, "No, no! Go away! We are closed!"

He ran out to jiggle the lock on the door, showing that he really meant to shut the place down. All the tables were empty and there was no one around. He had probably just been airing out the bar when I arrived.

"I've come about the parrot," I said.

"No, no," he cried, his eyes looking wet. "I won't talk. It's too much. If I were not Catholic, I would kill myself. Poor Papa. Poor El Córdoba!"

"El Córdoba?" I murmured.

"That," he said fiercely, "was the parrot's name!"

"Yes," I said, recovering quickly. "El Córdoba. I've come to rescue him."

That made him stop and blink. Shadows and then sunlight went over his face and then shadows again.

"Impossible! Could you? No, no. How could anyone! Who *are* you?"

"A friend to Papa and the bird," I said quickly. "And the more time we talk, the farther away goes the criminal. You want El Córdoba back tonight? Pour us several of Papa's good drinks and talk."

My bluntness worked. Not two minutes later, we were drinking Papa's special, seated in the bar near the empty place where the cage used to sit. The little man, whose name was Antonio, kept wiping that empty place and then wiping his eyes with the bar rag. As I finished the first drink and started on the second, I said:

"This is no ordinary kidnaping."

"You're telling me!" cried Antonio. "People came from all over the world to see that parrot, to talk to El Córdoba, to hear him, ah, God, speak with the voice of Papa. May his abductors sink and burn in hell, yes, hell."

"They will," I said. "Whom do you suspect?"

"Everyone. No one."

"The kidnaper," I said, eyes shut for a moment, savoring the drink, "had to be educated, a book reader, I mean, that's obvious, isn't it? Anyone like that around the last few days?"

"Educated. No education. *Señor*, there have always been strangers the last ten, the last twenty years, always asking for Papa. When Papa was here, they met him. With Papa gone, they met El Córdoba, the great one. So it was always strangers and strangers."

"But think, Antonio," I said, touching his trembling elbow. "Not only educated, a reader, but someone in the last few days who was—how shall I put it?—odd. Strange. Someone so peculiar, *muy eccéntrico*, that you remember him above all others. Someone who—"

"*¡Madre de Dios!*" cried Antonio, leaping up. His eyes stared off into memory. He seized his head as if it had just exploded. "Thank you, *señor*. *¡Si, si!* What a creature! In the name of Christ, there was such a one yesterday! He was very small. And he spoke like this:

very high—*eeeee*. Like a *muchacha* in a school play, eh? Like a canary swallowed by a witch! And he wore a blue-velvet suit with a big yellow tie."

"Yes, yes!" I had leaped up now and was almost yelling. "Go on!"

"And he had a small very round face, *señor*, and his hair was yellow and cut across the brow like this—*zitt!* And his mouth small, very pink, like candy, yes? He—he was like, yes, *uno muñeco*, of the kind one wins at carnivals."

"Kewpie dolls!"

"¡Sí! At Coney Island, yes, when I was a child, Kewpie dolls! And he was so high, you see? To my elbow. Not a midget, no—but—and how old? Blood of Christ, who can say? No lines in his face, but—thirty, forty, fifty. And on his feet he was wearing—"

"Green booties!" I cried.

"¿Qué?"

"Shoes, boots!"

"Sí." He blinked, stunned. "But how did you *know?*"

I exploded, "Shelley Capon!"

"That is the name! And his friends with him, *señor*, all laughing—no, giggling. Like the nuns who play basketball in the late afternoons near the church. Oh, *señor*, do you think that they, that he—"

"I don't think, Antonio, I *know*. Shelley Capon, of all the writers in the world, hated Papa. Of course he would snatch El Córdoba. Why, wasn't there a rumor once that the bird had memorized Papa's last, greatest, and as-yet-not-put-down-on-paper novel?"

"There was such a rumor, *señor*. But I do not write books, I tend bar. I bring crackers to the bird. I—"

"You bring me the phone, Antonio, please."

"You know where the bird is, *señor?*"

"I have the hunch beyond intuition, the big one. *Gracias*." I dialed the Havana Libre, the biggest hotel in town.

"Shelley Capon, please."

The phone buzzed and clicked.

Half a million miles away, a midget boy Martian lifted the receiver and played the flute and then the bell chimes with his voice: "Capon here."

"Damned if you aren't!" I said. And got up and ran out of the Cuba Libre bar.

Racing back to Havana by taxi, I thought of Shelley as I'd seen him before. Surrounded by a storm of friends, living out of suitcases, ladling soup from other people's plates, borrowing money from billfolds seized from your pockets right in front of you, counting the lettuce leaves with relish, leaving rabbit pellets on your rug, gone. Dear Shelley Capon.

Ten minutes later, my taxi with no brakes dropped me running and spun on to some ultimate disaster beyond town.

Still running, I made the lobby, paused for information, hurried upstairs, and stopped short before Shelley's door. It pulsed in spasms like a bad heart. I put my ear to the door. The wild calls and cries from inside might have come from a flock of birds, feather-stripped in a hurricane. I felt the door. Now it seemed to tremble like a vast laundromat that had swallowed and was churning an acid-rock group and a lot of very dirty linen. Listening, my underwear began to crawl on my legs.

I knocked. No answer. I touched the door. It drifted open. I stepped in upon a scene much too dreadful for Bosch to have painted.

Around the pigpen living room were strewn various life-size dolls, eyes half-cracked open, cigarettes smoking in burned, limp fingers, empty Scotch glasses in hands, and all the while the radio belted them with concussions of music broadcast from some Stateside asylum. The place was sheer carnage. Not ten seconds ago, I felt, a large dirty locomotive must have plunged through here. Its victims had been hurled in all directions and now lay upside down in various parts of the room, moaning for first aid.

In the midst of this hell, seated erect and proper, well dressed in velveteen jerkin, persimmon bow tie, and bottle-green booties, was, of course, Shelley Capon. Who with no surprise at all waved a drink at me and cried:

"I *knew* that was you on the phone. I am absolutely telepathic! Welcome, Raimundo!"

He always called me Raimundo. Ray was plain bread and butter. Raimundo made me a don with a breeding farm full of bulls. I let it be Raimundo.

"Raimundo, sit down! No . . . fling yourself into an *interesting* position."

"Sorry," I said in my best Dashiell Hammett manner, sharpening my chin and steeling my eyes. "No time."

I began to walk around the room among his friends Fester and Soft and Ripply and Mild Innocuous and some actor I remembered who, when asked how he would do a part in a film, had said, "I'll play it like a doe."

I shut off the radio. That made a lot of people in the room stir: I yanked the radio's roots out of the wall. Some people sat up. I raised a window. I threw the radio out. They all screamed as if I had thrown their mothers down an elevator shaft.

The radio made a satisfying sound on the cement sidewalk below. I turned, with a beatific smile on my face. A number of people were on their feet, swaying toward me with faint menace. I pulled a twenty-dollar bill out of my pocket, handed it to someone without looking at him, and said, "Go buy a new one." He ran out the door slowly. The door slammed. I heard him fall down the stairs as if he were after his morning shot in the arm.

"All right, Shelley," I said, "where is it?"

"Where is *what*, dear boy?" he said, eyes wide with innocence.

"You know what I mean." I stared at the drink in his tiny hand.

Which was a Papa drink, the Cuba Libre's very own